For Paul

the nicest pirate we know

LITTLE TIGER PRESS
An imprint of Magi Publications
1 The Coda Centre, 189 Munster Road, London SW6 6AW, UK
www.littletigerpress.com
First published in Great Britain 2003
First American edition published by Handprint Books 2003
This edition published 2010
Text and illustrations copyright © Diane and Christyan Fox 2003
Diane and Christyan Fox have asserted their rights to
be identified as the author and illustrator of this work
under the Copyright, Designs and Patents Act, 1988
All rights reserved · ISBN 978-1-84895-206-5
Printed in China · LTP/1800/0157/0910
2 4 6 8 10 9 7 5 3 1

Pirate PiggyWiggy

Christyan and Diane Fox

LITTLE TIGER PRESS

Sometimes when I sail my little boats, I dream of what it might be like to be a swashbuckling pirate!

I would wear
a big black hat,
a patch over my eye
and have a parrot
on my shoulder...

My ship would be the finest that ever sailed the seven seas.

At night-time we could sit around the fire singing sea songs...

Ten paces north...
eight paces south...

Shiver-me-timbers, X marks the spot!

The richest treasure ever seen...